A Runaway Donkey

D1513262

Roman stories linking with the History
National Curriculum.

First published in 1996 by Franklin Watts
Paperback edition published 1997
This edition 1998

Franklin Watts
96 Leonard Street
London EC2A 4RH

Franklin Watts Australia
14 Mars Road
Lane Cove
NSW 2006

Series editor: Paula Borton
Consultants: Joan Blyth, Dr Anne Millard
Designer: Kirstie Billingham

A CIP catalogue record for this book
is available from the British Library.

ISBN 0 7496 2631 3 (pbk)
0 7496 2332 2 (hbk)

Dewey Classification 937

Printed in Great Britain

A Runaway Donkey

by
Mick Gowar

Illustrations by Martin Remphry

W

FRANKLIN WATTS

LONDON • NEW YORK • SYDNEY

1

To Ostia

"Will we be there soon?" asked Livia.

Drusilla sighed. "You asked me that only five minutes ago," she said. "We'll be there when we're there."

"What a silly thing to say," thought Livia. She lifted the corner of the curtain

that surrounded the swaying litter in which
she and her mother were travelling.

"Don't do that," said Drusilla sharply.
"How many times must I tell you? It's
common to look out. And I want you to
be on your best behaviour today. Flavia
and her daughters are real ladies. And

Flavia will be expecting perfect manners from you!"

From the lifted corner of the curtain, Livia could just make out the front legs and brown chest of her father's horse trotting behind the litter.

"Livia!" Drusilla snapped. "Do as

you're told - for once!
Stop peeping!"

With a weary groan,
Livia let the curtain flap
flop down. It was so
boring being bumped
around on a litter.

"If only I was a boy,"
thought Livia, "I could
ride on a horse like father
and Great Uncle Titus.

Then I could see everything. Instead, I have to be cooped up like a chicken in a curtained box!"

"Look there!" she heard Uncle Titus exclaim. "Down that street - you can just see the docks!"

The docks! The famous Ostia harbour! Where ships came from all over the world, bringing cargoes of wine and grain and priceless spices and perfumes!

Livia excitedly lifted the curtain to look out.

"Livia! What have I told you!"

Livia let down the flap and slumped sullenly onto the embroidered cushions.

"This port is what the family business is all about," said Uncle Titus. "We grow olives and make oil and wine on the farm, but that's only a small part of the business. What we grow has to be sold and shipped anywhere in the world where oil and wine is needed - Gaul, Asia Minor, even Britain! But the ships don't come back empty, oh no. Most of the money I make is from what I bring *in* - spices and perfumed oils from the East, smoked hams and pottery from Gaul, statues and jewellery from Greece."

Lucius, Livia's father, did his best to look interested, but all he could think of was his aching bottom. He hadn't ridden

a horse in...he tried to remember - months
- years? He tried not to groan as he
joggled uncomfortably up and down on
the hard leather saddle.

"Yes, yes!" he grinned through clenched
teeth. "Very interesting, Uncle Titus.
Very interesting."

Lucius tried to grip harder with his knees to stop the joggling. But when he tried to grip, his sore thighs rubbed against the girth straps.

"Ooooh!" he couldn't stop a groan of pain. He stopped gripping and let himself be joggled roughly up and down instead. "Oooof!"

"Not used to riding - eh?" asked Uncle Titus with a grin.

"Err - just a little out of practice," admitted Lucius.

"A few more months and you'll be riding like a Scythian!" said Uncle Titus. "There's only one way, my boy. Ride every day - for at least two hours!"

Two hours! Lucius was appalled.

He gazed wistfully at the litter. "What I wouldn't give to be carried along in comfort!" he thought. "Oh! To be reclining on soft cushions instead of being bounced along like a sack of apples on the back of this chestnut brute!"

"*Halt!*" commanded Uncle Titus.

There was a lurch and a bump as the slaves put down the litter. At last, the

curtain was pulled back and Livia and her mother were lowered down onto the broad marble pavement. Livia stared all around her. She looked up at the enormous building in front of them. The pillars seemed to go up and up.

"Don't gawp, Livia!" Drusilla hissed.

Uncle Titus climbed down from his horse, helped by one of the slaves.

"Well, my dears, here we are - the baths!" he announced proudly, as though he had just finished building them with his own hands. "Your friends will be waiting for you inside. Lucius and I will spend the rest of the morning inspecting my warehouses. We will meet you at the *insula* this afternoon."

He turned back to his horse. The same slave who had helped him down, knelt and

cupped his hands to provide a step up.
Uncle Titus swung himself into the saddle
and turned to Lucius.

"Ready?" he asked.

Lucius gave a pained smile and
nodded.

"Off we go then!" said Uncle Titus cheerfully. He raised his arm and saluted Drusilla and Livia. "Have a pleasant morning," he called as the two men trotted off down the broad road towards the harbour.

Lucius couldn't resist a backward glance. "If only I was going for a nice, hot relaxing bath!" he thought. He groaned as his red, raw thighs scraped against the thick saddle strips.

"If only..."

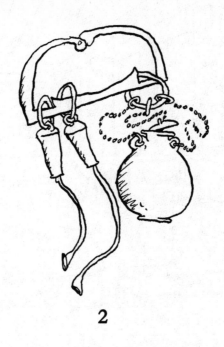

2

Livia Makes A Splash!

Livia was even more astonished by the inside of the bath house. The baths at Uncle Titus' villa were lovely, but these were *gorgeous*! She had never seen anything quite as beautiful as the glowing mosaic floors and the shimmering colours

of the wall paintings. It was like entering
a magic blue and green undersea world
of frolicking sea nymphs riding on the
backs of dolphins.

Everything would have been wonderful
if it hadn't been for her mother's cousin
Flavia and her two horrible daughters,

Julia and Antonia.

They had been waiting for Drusilla and Livia in the changing rooms. They were like three tall skinny birds - a family of storks, Livia thought when she saw them. All three had unnaturally pale, creamy white faces and long beaky noses.

Livia could feel the two girls looking her up and down. She was wearing her best tunic, but Livia could see by the way they looked down their noses, and then exchanged glances, that Julia and Antonia were not impressed. Livia looked at their milky white faces and then down at her own sunburnt arms. She felt awkward and clumsy and lumpy.

They all handed their clothes to the slaves and went into the *tepidarium*. Livia quite liked the tepidarium, because it wasn't too hot. But before she'd been able properly to enjoy the warmth, Flavia was leading them all into the *caldarium*, the hot room. The shock of the heat, even after the warmth of the tepidarium, made Livia gasp. She walked slowly to a bench and sat down beside Julia and Antonia.

No one said anything. Eventually, Julia, the older of the two girls, turned to Livia.

"Tell me, Livia..." she said in an over-polite, grown-up way. "Where do you live?"

"Erm, on my Great Uncle Titus' farm," Livia replied. She hoped it was the right answer.

Julia looked at Antonia, Antonia looked at Julia. Antonia sniffed. Livia knew that it *wasn't* the right answer. She felt herself

getting hotter, and it wasn't just from the heat of the caldarium.

"But we used to live in our own house in Verulamium," Livia added, hoping this would impress the two girls.

"Where's that?" asked Antonia.

"In Britain," Livia replied.

"Britain!" exclaimed Antonia. Julia and Antonia snorted. Britain was obviously the *last* place to live.

"We live in the *Garden House*," announced Julia proudly. "The most expensive apartments in the whole of Ostia. And we have our own personal slaves, don't we Antonia? Tell me, Livia, do you have your own personal slaves?"

"Yes!" said Livia angrily. "Lots and lots!"

The other two girls looked at each other and then back at Livia. They sat in silence for a long time as the bath-house slaves scraped them down with *strigils* and rubbed oil into their skin.

Livia could hear her mother saying loudly to Flavia, "Of course, we plan to buy a villa on the coast overlooking Capri soon. Living on a farm is alright for country people who don't know any better, but of course we *do* miss all the luxuries we're used to..."

Livia closed her eyes and tried to shut out the sound of her mother's voice. It was so embarrassing having to listen to Drusilla trying to be as grand as Flavia and her daughters.

At last it was time for the cold pool, the *frigidarium*. This was always Livia's favourite part of the bath. Although the cold water was a shock, it was *such* a relief to splash about after the heavy, humid heat of the caldarium.

Livia rushed to the side of the pool and jumped in. She let out a little shriek of delight as she came to the surface.

Slowly Livia realised that she was alone in the pool. She looked up. Her mother and Flavia were staring at her in shock and horror. Julia and Antonia were smirking.

Julia and Antonia lowered themselves gracefully inch by inch into the cold water.

"The sooner we get an apartment in a civilised town," Livia heard her mother say to Flavia, "the better it will be for Livia!"

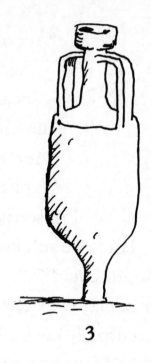

3

Lucius Learns A Lesson

Lucius leant dizzily against one of the *amphora*, the tall jars which were stacked against the brick walls of the warehouse.

"*Aaaaaaa-tchoo!*"

The enormous sneeze echoed through the dimly lit building.

"Aaaaat-choo!"
The second
sneeze boomed
up into the roof.
"Aaaaaat-choo!"
"Jupiter!"
"I'm sorry, Uncle
Titus. I don't know what's
wrong with - *Aaaat-choo!"*

"Mind your backs, your Lordships!"
Bleary-eyed and dazed, Lucius let Uncle
Titus steer him aside as a burly man in a
leather apron lumbered past them carrying
another amphora.

"I don't - *Aaaat-choo!"*

"Come on," said Uncle Titus, taking
Lucius' arm again. "We'd better get you
into the fresh air."

Half-blinded by the tears running from

his itchy eyes, Lucius followed
Uncle Titus towards the big
square of light at the far end
of the warehouse. They went
through the big doorway and
into the dazzling sunlight.

Lucius stood on the wooden jetty, breathing deeply. After a minute or two the itching in his eyes became less, and the burning feeling at the back of his nose stopped. He looked out at the harbour. Along both sides of the harbour were warehouses like his Uncle's, with wooden jettys and walkways. At almost every jetty a boat was tied up. Powerful, muscular slaves bustled from the ships to the warehouses and from the warehouses to the ships lugging enormous amphorae.

"Feeling better?" asked Uncle Titus.

Lucius took a deep breath. "Yes, thank you," he replied. "I do apologise, Uncle Titus. I don't understand what came over me.

Maybe I'm sickening for something?"

Uncle Titus shook his head. "Spices," he said, "and oils."

Lucius looked at him, puzzled.

"The cargo being unloaded this morning is spices and oils from the East," explained Uncle Titus.

Lucius sniffed.

"I once had a Greek clerk who had the same trouble," Uncle Titus continued.

"The smell of spices and oils made him sneeze and sneeze. I had to sell him on to someone who was looking for a tutor. A pity, he was a good man." Uncle Titus shook his head sadly.

The two men stared out across the harbour in silence.

Suddenly, there was a crashing sound to their left, followed by another and another. Lucius looked along the harbour to the next warehouse. Outside, on the wooden jetty, two slaves were deliberately smashing up amphorae with wooden hammers.

"Should they be doing that?" asked Lucius.

Uncle Titus followed Lucius' pointing finger.

"Ballast," he said.

"Pardon?"

"They're breaking up empty amphorae for ballast - that means something to weight down the ship," explained Uncle Titus. "You see, ships are built to carry cargoes, and they sail best when they're carrying something. That ship on the jetty

has to go back empty. But if it sailed empty it wouldn't be stable - it would be too light and could easily turn over and capsize. So they're going to weight it down with broken amphorae."

Lucius watched the slaves breaking up the amphorae. "There's so much about the business I don't know," he thought gloomily.

"We'll have to go back in," said Uncle Titus. "I *must* check all the cargoes." He led the way back through the doorway and into the dark warehouse. "The world is full of cheats and rogues," he said. "And the biggest thieves are always the ones who are working for you!"

As they walked slowly down the centre of the gloomy building, Lucius felt his eyes and nose start to itch again.

"Oh dear," he thought. "How am I ever going to help run the business, when every time I go near a cargo I - I - I - "

He closed his eyes tightly and held his breath. But it was no good.

"*Aaaaaa- aaaaaa....AAAAT-CHOO!*"

4

The Runaway Donkey

"How *could* you?" snapped Drusilla, as
soon as she and Livia were back in the
privacy of the litter. "Showing me up like
that! Jumping into the pool like a - like a-"
Drusilla searched for the right word,
"Like a common farm-girl!"

Livia stared morosely at the curtains.

"And look at me when I'm speaking to you!"

Liva turned over to face her mother, but wouldn't look her in the eyes.

"And when we get to their apartment, you're to be quiet and chat nicely to Julia and Antonia, and not rush around."

Livia sighed. Until she'd met the two girls, she'd been looking forward to playing

knucklebones or whipping-tops - playing *something*. But now she was sure that Julia and Antonia didn't play anything at all. They probably *did* spend all their time sitting quietly so their beautiful tunics didn't get creased!

The litter stopped, and there was a jolt as it was put down.

"We must be there," said Drusilla. "Remember, Livia - your very, *very* best behaviour."

They were helped out of the litter by the slaves. Just ahead of them was the magnificent gilded litter of Flavia.

They had stopped in front of a large square building, standing like an island

surrounded on all sides by roads. On the street level were shops. Livia could see the delicate almond cakes and succulent honey cakes on the wooden counter of the baker's. In the shop next door were piles of

apples, figs - and mounds of several fruit Livia didn't know.

But up above the shops...! Livia stared open-mouthed. The building seemed to reach right up into the sky! Livia tried to count the floors - two, three, four, five, six... She began to feel dizzy gazing up. And on each level were balconies, and on the balconies were pots of flowers and shrubs. There were hundreds and hundreds of blooms going up and up, layer after layer, as far as Livia could see.

"Don't stare like that Livia," snapped Drusilla. "Anyone would think you'd never seen an *insula* before!"

She said it in a voice which seemed too loud to Livia. Livia looked round and saw that Flavia, Julia and Antonia were standing behind her. They were all looking

down their long noses disdainfully.

"This is where we live," announced Flavia, "the Garden House Insula."

Two slaves were already waiting for them at the doorway to the building. Another two had hurried ahead to make sure that everything was ready for their mistresses' arrival.

"This way -" said Flavia.

But before anyone could move there

was a loud bellowing, braying noise from out on the street.

"Watch out, my ladies!" shouted one of the litter slaves.

A donkey with two baskets of apples tied across his back suddenly lashed out with his back legs, hitting a corner of the litter.

"You devil!" shrieked the man who had been leading the donkey. "I'll show you who's boss!"

He hit the donkey with the stick he was carrying. Julia and Antonia squealed with fright, as the donkey gave another bellowing *hee-haw* and kicked back again with his hooves.

"Brute!" yelled the man, and hit the donkey again.

This time, the donkey's violent bucking caused the apples to fall out of the baskets on his back. Apples cascaded onto the road and began to roll into the gutters.

Three ragged children, who had been watching from the opposite pavement, ran across the road and began grabbing handfuls of fallen apples.

"Get off my apples, you vermin!"
roared the donkey man, lashing out at the
children with his stick.

The donkey, suddenly unburdened,
bolted forward. The two slaves by the door
dived aside as the donkey galloped through
the front door of the Garden House.

"Stop it, someone!" yelled Flavia.

Livia ran forward to see what would happen next.

"Not you, Livia!" shouted Drusilla, but Livia was already in the front hall. There was no sign of the donkey, but there was the sound of shouting and screaming coming from the floor above.

Livia leapt up the broad stairs. As she reached the first floor landing, she saw the back of the donkey as it swerved to the right and galloped through the open door of an apartment. There were more screams, cries and shouts, followed by several loud crashes and *hee-haws*. Then silence.

Livia waited a minute or two, then cautiously went up to the open door and looked in.

Inside was a magnificent apartment

with a mosaic floor and painted walls.
Peeping out from behind the pillars that
surrounded the apartment, Livia could see
three or four frightened-looking faces.

Immediately in front of her were the remains of several vases which had been smashed to pieces. In the centre of the apartment was what had once been a magnificent indoor garden, but most of the pots had been knocked over and smashed.

In the middle of the garden, looking quite calm after its adventure, stood the donkey. He was peacefully chewing the leaves from a potted fig tree that was lying on its side.

"What a mess!" thought Livia.

"Oi-you!" hissed a voice. Livia turned to see a bald-headed slave peering out from behind one of the pillars. "Is that your donkey?"

"No," said Livia.

"It's not a donkey, it's a demon!" said a frightened female voice from behind another pillar.

"What are we going to do?" wailed a third.

Livia crept slowly forward, narrowly avoiding a large pile of fresh donkey dung.

"Hello," she said. "Don't worry, I'm not going to hurt you."

The donkey looked up, nervously.

"Whoah," Livia said soothingly. "Whoaaaah."

She reached forward and picked up the dangling rope which was tied round the donkey's neck.

She gently tugged on the rope, and the donkey took a step towards her.

"There, there," Livia murmured, reaching out and stroking the donkey between the ears. "Who's a good boy..."

"Are you *sure* that's not your donkey?" asked the bald-headed man suspiciously.

"No," said Livia, "but there are donkeys on my uncle's farm. They're nothing to be afraid of."

But the slaves clearly didn't believe her, and stayed safely behind their pillars.

Slowly, Livia led the donkey out of the wrecked apartment.

As Livia and the donkey reached the landing, the donkey man came puffing up the stairs.

"There you are, you monster!" he growled at the donkey. Then he looked at

Livia. "Er...thanks for catching him, Miss."

Livia looked down the stairs and gulped. "How are we going to get him down there?" she asked.

The donkey man laughed. "That's no bother for a donkey, Miss," he replied. Donkeys can climb anything. They can climb up and down sheer mountainsides. You saw how fast he came up, didn't you?"

They led the clopping donkey down the stone stairs and out onto the street.

"*Livia!*" Drusilla grabbed her by the shoulders. "Why did you run in there? You could have been hurt! Are you alright?" Livia grinned. "*I'm* alright," she replied, "but you should see the apartment up on the first floor!" She paused. She was suddenly aware that Flavia, Julia and Antonia were staring at her.

They looked even paler than normal.

"Did you say...the *first* floor?" asked Flavia in a small voice.

"Yes," said Livia cheerfully. "The apartment on the right. There are plants knocked over, vases smashed - a complete wreck!"

Flavia closed her eyes. She swayed slightly, then pulled herself together. "I suppose I should thank you, Livia, for helping to get the donkey out." She paused and took a couple of deep breaths.

She turned to Livia's mother. "I'm sure you will excuse me, Drusilla, if I do *not* invite you to lunch today," she said with great politeness. "But I don't believe our apartment will be...." She seemed lost for words. "Fit to entertain in."

Drusilla looked confused. "I-I don't understand."

Flavia took another deep breath. "Our apartment," she looked down her long nose at Livia, "is on the first floor, on the right!"

"How *could* you, Livia!" scolded Drusilla when they were bumping along in the litter. "How could you have laughed like that! To have your beautiful home destroyed by a - by a - *donkey*! It's dreadful! Those poor girls were so upset -

and all you could do was laugh like a common street urchin! I'm ashamed of you!" She glared at Livia. "I wouldn't be surprised if Flavia never invites us to lunch again! You'll be sorry then - won't you?"

But there was something about Livia's broad grin that made Drusilla think that Livia *wouldn't* be sorry at all!

Roman Town Life

Ostia

Ostia was the port of the city of Rome and was one of the biggest trading centres in the Roman Empire. It was on the coast, at the mouth of the River Tiber, about 80 kilometres from Rome. Many of the goods which came into Ostia were first stored in warehouses, like Uncle Titus'. They were then taken up the Tiber by barge to Rome. The barges would often be pulled up the river by teams of slaves.

Insula

This word means 'island' and
was the Latin name for the big
apartment buildings in which a
lot of the people of Ostia,
Rome and other big cities lived.
By the fourth century, there
were 46,000 insulae in Rome
alone! Many of them were not
very well built or safe. Laws

were passed to try and stop the buildings being
over 20 metres high, but many builders ignored
them. There were usually shops on the ground floor
and flights of stairs leading up to the apartments.

Baths

Roman baths were like the saunas we have today.
Instead of soaping themselves in tubs of hot water,
the Romans would sit in very hot rooms and sweat
all the dirt away. The sweat and the grime would
then be scraped off by slaves with objects known as

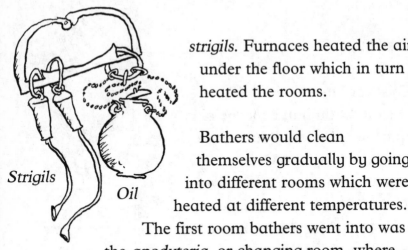

Strigils

Oil

strigils. Furnaces heated the air under the floor which in turn heated the rooms.

Bathers would clean themselves gradually by going into different rooms which were heated at different temperatures. The first room bathers went into was the *apodyteria*, or changing room, where they would leave their clothes. The next room was called the *tepidarium* which was kept quite warm. Then came the hot room, or the *caldarium*, and finally the cold room, or the *frigidarium*, where there would be a large pool that bathers could plunge into.